Miles Of Smiles
The Story of Roxey, the Long Island Rail Road Dog

By Heather Hill Worthington
Illustrated by Bill Farnsworth

Mile Of Smiles
The Story of Roxey, the Long Island Rail Road Dog

Text copyright © 2010 by Heather Hill Worthington
Illustrations copyright © 2010 by Bill Farnsworth

Blue Marlin Publications, Ltd.
823 Aberdeen Road, West Bay Shore, NY 11706
www.bluemarlinpubs.com

Printed and bound in China by Regent Publishing Services, Ltd.
May 2010
Job # 100356

Book design & layout by Jude T. Rich

Library of Congress Cataloging-in-Publication Data

Worthington, Heather Hill.
  Miles of smiles : the story of Roxey, the Long Island Rail Road dog / by Heather Hill Worthington ; illustrated by Bill Farnsworth.
     p. cm.
  Summary: Tells the story of Roxey, a stray dog that became the mascot of the Long Island Rail Road between 1901 and 1915, even meeting President Theodore Roosevelt. Based on a true story; includes author's notes with facts about Roxey and the history of the Long Island Rail Road.
  ISBN 978-0-9792918-4-5 (alk. paper); ISBN 978-0-9792918-8-3 (softcover : alk. paper)
 [1. Dogs--Fiction. 2. Long Island Rail Road Company--Fiction. 3. Railroads--Fiction. 4. Long Island (N.Y.)--History--20th century--Fiction.] I. Farnsworth, Bill, ill. II. Title.
  PZ7.W8882Mi 2010
  [E]--dc22
                    2010004287

Blue Marlin Publications, Ltd.
823 Aberdeen Road, West Bay Shore, NY 11706
www.bluemarlinpubs.com

Author's Notes

Roxey

Roxey was a real dog who did travel the Long Island Rail Road for 15 years, from 1901 through 1915. Thanks to train workers and passengers who cared for him, Roxey remained healthy and well fed throughout his long life. Agent Heaney was the real name of Roxey's station agent master. Records show that Agent Heaney renewed Roxey's dog license regularly, even after Roxey became the Long Island Rail Road mascot.

Newspapers kept tabs on Roxey and recorded sightings. On July 9, 1911, *The New York Times* reported: "Roxey, the Long Island Rail Road mascot, is the subject of more stories of adventure and interest than you can count hairs to his yellow hide." In another account, Roxey was spotted riding the elevators alone at Penn Station in New York City. Reportedly, Roxey did travel to Philadelphia and back once, but then he never rode anything but the Long Island Rail Road again.

A favorite story of trainmen was the one in which Roxey met President Theodore Roosevelt. In yet another, Roxey looked for a lady carrying a parasol because she had come close to adopting him.

Roxey had many friends, but he was particularly drawn to those wearing the Long Island Rail Road uniform. He followed train workers home for supper and often spent the night in their homes. One very special friend of Roxey's was Elsa Hess, a school teacher living in Merrick who cared for injured and stray animals. After Roxey died of old age, it was Miss Hess who arranged for a headstone to be placed on Roxey's grave at the Merrick train station. The marker, which can still be found there, reads: "Roxey LIRR Dog." For years after his death, Roxey's many friends left flowers there as a special way to remember him.

President Theodore Roosevelt

Theodore Roosevelt, the 26th President of the United States, was in office from 1901 to 1909, while Roxey was riding the rails. He was a busy man. His home, named Sagamore Hill, in Oyster Bay, Long Island, was called the "Summer White House." There, he lived with his second wife, Edith, and their six children. The children had many pets and were fond of the outdoors like their father. When the President traveled home from Washington D.C., big celebrations, like the one in this book, were planned just to welcome him. The President often used the word "bully," which in those days meant, "Fine! Excellent! Well done!"

The Long Island Rail Road

The Long Island Rail Road began in 1834. During Roxey's tenure on the rails, extensive improvements were made. The western part of the system was electrified. Steel passenger cars came into use. Four tunnels were constructed under the East River. By 1910, the large terminal in New York City, Pennsylvania Station, was finished. This station is among the most famous in the world. In the past 100 years, Long Island has grown and grown, and so has the LIRR. Today, this railroad is the busiest commuter railroad in North America, with approximately 81 million passengers riding every year. Imagine how many friends Roxey would have if he were commuting from Long Island to New York City on the LIRR today!

Acknowledgements

The Author would like to express her gratitude to everyone who supported her efforts in writing this story. She would like to especially acknowledge the late Dr. John Allen Gable of the Theodore Roosevelt Association, for his early support of this book; LIRR expert and author, Ron Ziel, for giving his expert opinion regarding questions about the LIRR; and LIRR Historical Society President, Dave Morrison, for sharing his "Roxie" postcard, which was used as a model in Bill Farnsworth's paintings.

Dedications

To my family — Heather Hill Worthington

For Katie — Bill Farnsworth

August 1901
Long Island, New York

A late afternoon thunderstorm rolled
into the Garden City Train Station,
frightening a wet, yellow dog.

Boom-boom-boom rumbled the thunder.

Lightning flashed!

The dog barked and barked, wanting to
be let inside the station house.
Still, nobody came.

Finally, the door did open, and a tall man in a blue uniform looked down at him. "Whose dog are you?" he asked. "Don't you have a home?"

The dog burst into the empty waiting room. Inside the man's office, he curled up under the telegraph desk.

The agent spoke softly to him. "I once had a dog like you, afraid of thunderstorms. If nobody claims you, then you can be my new station dog. I'll call you Roxey, after my old dog," Agent Heaney said.

And just like that, this Roxey found a home with Agent Heaney in Hempstead. Each morning, the two commuted to work on the train. Roxey had so much fun riding to and from Garden City, but he wasn't the kind of dog who liked lazing around a station all day long.

While Agent Heaney worked, tending to passengers' needs, Roxey wasn't allowed to ride on any trains. Roxey grew restless. He wasn't even allowed to ride on the baggage wagon.

Sometimes Roxey followed passengers to the big hotel across the street. He thought nothing of crossing the wide boulevard, startling horses, or dodging motorcars.

One day at the station, a lady holding a parasol shared her sandwich with him. Roxey followed her onto a departing train.

Whoo-hooooooooo!

The train left Garden City with Roxey on it.

"Aren't you Heaney's dog?" asked Frank, the conductor.

When Frank punched passengers' tickets, Roxey followed him down the aisle. Roxey peeked inside the engine cab and met Ed, the engineer.

"Aren't you Heaney's dog?" asked Ed. "Let me show you how I walk a dog!" he said, grinning. Ed put his hand on the throttle. The train sped faster and faster.

Roxey rested his paws on the window sill and sniffed the grassy meadows. A wild wind swept his face. Never had he felt so free!

He forgot that he was a station dog. He forgot that Agent Heaney worried. Roxey forgot about all the rules!

When Roxey returned to Garden City, Agent Heaney scolded him. "You have to stay put. You could get hurt!" he yelled.

Roxey sulked under a shade tree. Why did his master want to spoil all the fun? Soon, Frank the conductor found him.

Roxey wagged his tail.

Frank had a present for Roxey from all his new pals, the train workers. It was a special collar with a silver plate that read:
$$\text{I AM ROXEY}$$
$$\text{THE RAILROAD DOG}$$
$$\text{WHOSE DOG ARE YOU?}$$

"Now you don't have to worry," Frank told Agent Heaney. "We'll all look after Roxey."

But Agent Heaney wasn't amused. "Roxey's train hopping is going to get me fired!" he said.

"All aboard!" called Frank, when his train was ready to leave.

Roxey scrambled up the steps without Agent Heaney seeing him. The train left Garden City, puffing out clouds of smoke. Roxey was hooked on riding. He could not stop!

He changed trains at Jamaica.

Traveling to Merrick, Roxey sat with a school teacher.

Catching the Cannonball Express, he zipped – lickity-split – out east to Montauk.

He rode ocean waves, sniffed salt air breezes, and rested high upon the sand dunes.

Arriving in Greenport the next day, he spun on the engine turntable, dizzy with pleasure!

Maybe he wasn't cut out to be a station dog.

Roxey railroaded back to Garden City. There, Agent Heaney spoke to his boss, who was the President of the Long Island Rail Road.

Roxey didn't want to make trouble. He wanted to make friends. He stared Mr. Peters right in the eye and offered him his paw to shake.

Mr. Peters gave him a big, pleased-to-meet-you smile. "If Roxey insists on train hopping, I'm going to have to make him the railroad's official mascot," he said.

And just like that, Roxey got a ticket to ride the Long Island Rail Road. Any time he wanted. Anywhere he wanted. Roxey could ride all day and all night.

Best of all, he was given "rights" over all passengers and employees. He could sit on any seat on any train.

Roxey liked his bright, shiny rail pass. He stepped more quickly now.

"It's good luck to sit with Roxey," passengers said.

Roxey's dog license jingled as he traveled on every branch line. He still visited Agent Heaney, but he slept wherever he pleased. He dined with passengers in parlor cars. He even played with the children.

Roxey was the perfect mascot. He spread miles of smiles!

Roxey became so popular that the train workers collected money for him. They opened a bank account in his name. At one time, he had $300. The money was used to pay his veterinarian bills. A railroad dog does suffer mishaps.

Once, Roxey had a run-in with a motorcar. Another time he was struck by a bicycle. Yet another time, he was forced to duck under a passing train! Miraculously, he emerged unhurt.

And, still, he loved his life as a railroad dog.

One day something happened that made Roxey more than just a local mascot. He was in Long Island City when he spied a special train.

He saw a sign: RESERVED. He ducked under a rope to investigate. He passed another sign: PRIVATE.

Inside an empty train car, he saw a comfy bed. Roxey curled up on the bedcovers.

"Scram!" shouted a porter.

But Roxey refused to budge.

Along came his friend, Frank, the conductor. "The dog stays. Company rules," Frank told the porter.

Roxey sniffed the carnation pinned to Frank's uniform. Something strange was going on, and he knew it!

The porter shouted again. "This car is reserved for THE PRESIDENT OF THE UNITED STATES!"

Then in strode the man himself, President Theodore Roosevelt. He was a bear of a man with a bushy mustache. "What's all the fuss about?" asked the President, straightening his spectacles.

"It's the dog. He's on your bed, sir," said the porter.

Roxey sat up.

"This dog has a rail pass, sir," explained Frank. "Roxey is the pet of all the trainmen."

"By Jove. He does have a rail pass!" said the President. "I am in favor of standing up for one's rights. Two very important passengers can share one, private business car...Bully for Roxey!" the President declared.

Roxey and President Roosevelt railroaded to Oyster Bay.

Townspeople waited at the station.

From the back of the train, the President waved.

Roxey stood proudly next to him.

A band played *The Star-Spangled Banner*.

Schoolchildren waved flags.

Roxey wagged his tail, but at first nobody noticed him.

Guns saluted next. It was much too noisy at this station.

Boom-boom-boom!

It sounded just like a thunderstorm. Roxey barked.

Finally, the noise did stop.

Now when Roxey barked, everyone looked at him.

"Bully for Roxey!" the President declared.

"Bully for Roxey!" echoed the People, cheering just for him.

For fifteen years, Roxey traveled on the Long Island Rail Road. He met many more interesting folks.

In one town, he even posed for a picture postcard. Soon, passengers mailed the postcards far away.

Stories about Roxey appeared in newspapers and magazines. Roxey was a celebrity. Even so, he never forgot his special friends—especially Agent Heaney.

Whenever Roxey stepped off the train in Garden City, Agent Heaney welcomed him home.